The l

MW01101882

Story Keeper Series
Book 18

Dave and Pat Sargent (*left*) are longtime residents of Prairie Grove, Arkansas. Dave, a fourth-generation dairy farmer, began writing in early December of 1990. Pat, a former teacher, began writing in the fourth grade. They enjoy the outdoors and have a real love for animals.

Sue Rogers (*right*) returned to her beloved Mississippi after retirement. She shared books with children for more than thirty years. These stories fulfill a dream of writing books—to continue the sharing.

The Bundle Keeper

Story Keeper Series
Book 18

Dave and Pat Sargent
and Sue Rogers

Beyond "The End"
By Sue Rogers

Illustrated by Jane Lenoir

Ozark Publishing, Inc.
P.O. Box 228
Prairie Grove, AR 72753

Cataloging-in-Publication Data

Sargent, Dave, 1941–
  The bundle keeper / by Dave and Pat Sargent
and Sue Rogers ; illustrated by Jane Lenoir. —
Prairie Grove, AR : Ozark Publishing, c2005.
    p. cm. (Story keeper series ; 18)

    "Be responsible"—Cover.
    SUMMARY: Elzvee was learning about the
stars—Sun, Moon, Morning Star, Evening Star,
four that hold up the heavens, and all the others.
    ISBN 1-56763-937.2 (hc)
            1-56763-938-0 (pbk)
    1. Indians of North America—Juvenile
fiction. 2. Pawnee Indians—Juvenile fiction.
[1. Native Americans—United States—Fiction.
2. Pawnee Indians—Fiction.] 1. Sargent,
Pat, 1936– II. Rogers, Sue, 1933– III. Lenoir,
Jane, 1950– ill. IV. Title. V. Series.

    PZ7.S243Bu 2005
    [Fic]—dc21   2003090098

Printed in the United States of America

Inspired by

Pawnee medicine, which the Pawnees call power, and white people call faith.

Dedicated to

Elders Ewing, Johnson, McCutcheon, and Moak, Sue's teachers of faith.

Foreword

A fire burns in the center of a Pawnee girl's earth lodge. The rising smoke that goes through the opening above takes with it her prayers to Tirawa. Her name is Elzvee. Her father is the medicine man. She learns the powers of the sacred medicine bundle her father uses to guide and protect her people. Then she is asked to protect the bundle!

Contents

If you would like to have the authors of the Story Keeper Series visit your school, free of charge, just call us at 1-800-321-5671 or 1-800-960-3876.

Dear Reader,

Come back with me 150 years...
You are a young child living in a sea of waving grass. Wherever you might stand, you are in the center of a big circle and the blue sky touches the far prairie around you.

You laugh and run and play. You go in and out of the tall tunnel entrance to your home. It opens in the direction of Morning Star, where Sun rises. Sun sets in the direction of Evening Star. On that inside wall hangs a sacred bundle and buffalo skull. The sacred bundle holds the gifts of corn and buffalo. Four posts hold up your strong roof of thatch and mud and sod, like the four stars that hold up the heavens.

A fire burns in the center of your home. It cooks your food and makes you warm. The rising smoke that goes through the opening above takes with it your prayers to Tirawa. Tirawa-Atius, the Power Above, is above you.

1

When the sky fills with stars at night, you and your family go out to sit on the roof of your house and gaze up at them. You hear stories of how the stars created boys and girls. You see the Great Chief Star that never moves and watch the rest of the stars circle around him. There are many stories about the stars. They teach how things came to be. They tell how to cooperate with each other, and how important unity is among your people.

Come! Take this imaginary journey and meet my Pawnee grandmother, many grand-mothers back. Her name was Elzvee. Her father was a "medicine man". He was not a doctor like we have today, although a part of his job was to heal the sick. He had great power and influence.

With love,
Ellen

One

Medicine Man

There were forty dome-shaped earth lodges in our village. They were all very large lodges, where many people live—except one. It was mine. My family's lodge was small where only my parents, grand-mother, and I lived.

In the big lodges, there were more children than adults. The chil-dren played together. They shared secrets and explored the prairie together. They had grandparents and uncles and aunts to tell them stories. Their lodges were always filled with laughter, peace, and happiness.

3

There was peace and happiness in our lodge, but there was little laughter. There were no playmates. But there was Grandmother. She shared her food bowl with me and made sure I was safe and warm. In our hearts, we were one.

Our earth lodge was small by choice. It was built like the big ones. The walls were dirt. Tree trunks stood around the circle to support the earth-covered roof.

Four taller tree trunks outlined the hearth in the center.

The one on the east was painted red to represent the rising sun. The south was yellow for victory and the west was black for the setting sun. The north was white for the strength and purity of Pawnee beliefs.

We slept along the outside walls. The west wall was the sacred area. Father was the priest (medicine man) for our village. He carefully watched the stars through the smoke hole and entrance of our earth lodge.

From this watch, my father set the time for our cycle of planting, harvest, and hunting. Father held special ceremonies to secure the favor of Tirawa for every important event in the life of my people.

Grandmother said, "Your father has special duties at the first thunder in the spring, the planting of corn, on a buffalo hunt, and at the return of a war party. The spirits he brings, the animals that give him power, and the magical places where strange things are done—all are a part of your father's medicine."

Two

Moccasin Woman

Father was told in a vision how to make the tribal medicine bundle. Each of the powers he had been in contact with was in the bundle. It had powers of protection from harm or evil. It provided safety and success on trips of hunting or warfare. It had great healing powers.

The tribal medicine bundle was opened only at special times. If it was not opened just right it would not be sacred anymore. The proper people had to be there. It was an important part of Pawnee ceremonies.

My father was in charge of the medicine bundle. He knew the sacred uses of the bundle. He was the Bundle Keeper.

My mother helped my father with ritual ceremonies. Grandmother was proud of her daughter's honor.

"Always remember, my little Elzvee, breath is the blessing of life. Words are spoken with breath so they are sacred and must be used with care," Grandmother said.

My grandmother was a good example. Her words were always kind. So were her actions. If one of the women in our village was sick or having troubles, Grandmother cared for the woman's family and took the woman's duties.

Fresh buffalo meat, corn, or enough tanned leather for a pair of moccasins was often payment to Grandmother for her help. She cooked her food gifts. There were stacks of leather by her sleeping space.

The making and repair of moccasins was a never-ending job

for women. People needed a soft pair to wear inside the lodge. A harder type was needed for work and hunting. So Grandmother had become the village "moccasin

woman." She cut, then stitched and decorated the moccasins.

Making moccasins was Grandmother's way of being useful. I loved to sit at her feet, watching her slender fingers working. It taught me to cut and sew. A song or story always came when Grandmother and I were working together. She told of the deeds of our young men and of ghosts and spirits and animals.

"There are four directions— south, west, north, and east," my grandmother said as she took a stitch. "There are four parts in everything that grows from the earth. There are roots, stem, leaves, and fruit. And there are four kinds of creatures—those that swim, those that crawl, those that walk, and those that fly. Do you know the times that we measure our lives by, Elzvee?" she asked.

"Yes, I do know, Grandmother!" I said. "There are four—the night, the day, the moon, and the seasons. And there are four seasons, too. I have passed through five summers, Grandmother. That is why I am big enough now to help you with the moccasins."

"You are right, my heart of hearts," said Grandmother. "And that is why your mother and father want you to go with them on the next hunt. You will see how important they are in calling the buffalo. And you will get to live in a tipi."

"I need a new hoe for my garden work. Will you bring me a shoulder blade from a buffalo, child?" asked Grandmother.

"Yes, Grandmother," I said. "I shall miss you, Grandmother. Will you have new stories to tell me when I return?"

"Oh, you will have many stories to tell me," Grandmother said. She smiled and gave me a hug. I hugged her back.

"I won't be far away, Elzvee," said Grandmother. "Each night when you look up at the stars, remember that I will be looking at the same stars."

Three

Evening Star

On the trip to the hunting grounds, I rode with my mother on her horse some of the time. Other times I rode on the travois that held our packed tipi and supplies. I liked riding with my mother best. She told me things that would be happening.

"When your father decides where the buffalo herd might be, the hunt chief will send scouts," said my mother. "The scouts always paint their faces white like the wolf. They do this because they know the wolf's power will help them in their search for the buffalo."

The tipi was smaller than our lodge, but it was good. We went outside to gaze at the stars after dark.

"Evening Star is bright tonight," said Mother. "Evening Star has four messengers—clouds, winds, thunder, and lightening. Has she sent you a message, Elzvee?"

"Yes, Mother," I said. "Today I saw Grandmother in a cloud. She is safe in our earth lodge."

And so the days and nights went. Buffalo herds were located. The hunters had great success. The women worked the harvest of the hunt into food, tools, and clothing. It was time to pack and return to our village. There would be plenty of meat for the winter.

The gardens would be ready for harvest when we got back. There would be corn for everyone.

"Tell me about the men stars and women stars, Father," I said.

Father was watching the stars with Mother and me.

"Tirawa gave the stars great power," Father said. "Morning Star and Sun were placed in the east. They are men. In the west were those stars like women, Evening Star and Moon."

"Morning Star and Evening Star married and had a daughter. Sun and Moon married and had a son. So the human race was made. All was well until Coyote stole a sack of storms and brought evils into the world. We have been given sacred bundles by the heavenly powers to help us over- come these evils."

We began moving before sun- rise the next day. At the head of a canyon, someone shouted orders for the women, children, and pack ponies to take cover. One of our ene- mies was ready to attack our hunting party.   Suddenly their war whoop sounded. It was answered with a cry from the Pawnee warriors as they hurled themselves at the enemy.

Our warriors fought bravely, but their hunting bows were no match for the guns of the enemy. There were four of them for each Pawnee.

All at once Father was by my side. He swung me up and lashed me to his horse's body. He bound the sacred bundle to my back.

"Take care of this bundle and it will take care of you," Father said as he smacked his horse. The horse ran right into the noise and confusion of the battle.

I heard the whistle of bullets and arrows and shouts as we ran through the canyon. On and on the horse ran.

Battle sounds changed to songs of birds and ripples of water. I opened my eyes. The horse was drinking from a stream.

The horse began to run again. On and on!

Was I dreaming? Arms that could only belong to Grandmother were hugging me! Father's horse had brought me back to our village.

"I lost your buffalo shoulder blade, Grandmother," I sobbed. "But I will help you harvest the garden." My grandmother's arms tightened around me.

A few more people straggled in. My parents never came.

The bundle did take care of me, just as Father had said. I took care of it and later passed it to my daughter. But the ritual use of it was lost with my father, because only he had known the proper way to open it.

Four

Pawnee Facts

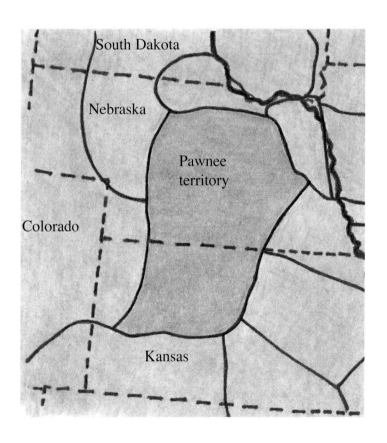

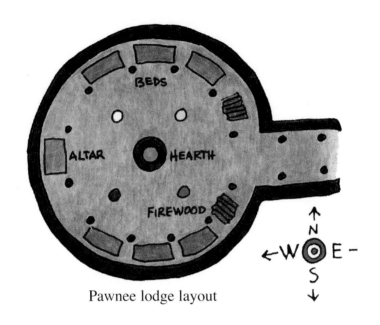

BEDS

ALTAR　HEARTH

FIREWOOD

N
←W ◉ E -
S
↓

Pawnee lodge layout

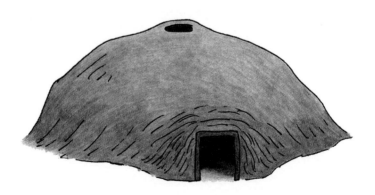

Pawnee dirt lodge

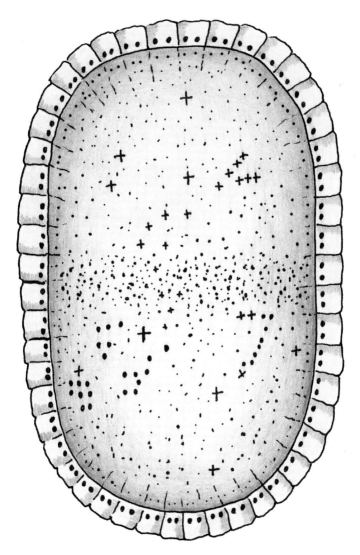

Pawnee star chart painted on leather

33

Pawnee moccasin

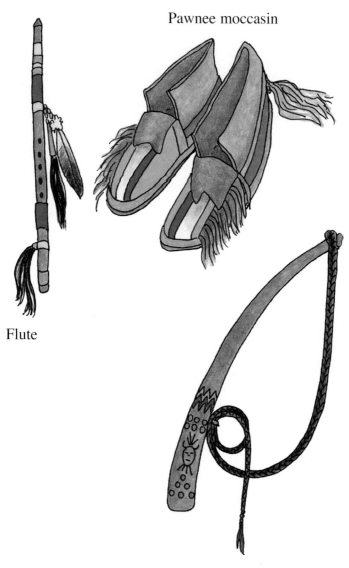

Flute

Pawnee whip

Silver arm bands

Choker-bone

Hair pipe breast plate made
of bone, leather, and beads

Flint knife with
deer antler haft

Pawnee dancer

Beyond "The End"

● Elzvee received a message from one of Evening Star's messengers (clouds) telling her that her grandmother was safe at home. Think about something you would like the clouds to see for you and bring you the message. Think about something you would like the wind to feel for you and bring you the message. Think about something you would like the thunder to hear and bring you the message. Think about something you would like lightening to bring to you. Write about all your messages from Evening Star.

CURRICULUM CONNECTIONS

● Observing stars is an activity that anyone can do with no special equipment other than the human eye. Can you locate Evening Star, Morning Star, and Great Chief Star? (HINT: Evening Star is our planet Venus; Morning Star is Mars; and Great Chief Star is Polaris, the North Star.)

● Elzvee was going to help harvest the gardens. Learn about the fun of gardening and how-to at the Kids Valley Garden website <www.raw-connections.com/garden>.

● There were 1,000 people in Elzvee's village. If each ate 2 pounds of meat daily, how much meat was needed to feed all the people? How many pounds are in a ton? Would they eat a ton of meat?

● If a 1,000 pound buffalo when butchered produced 450 pounds of fresh meat, how many buffalo would it take per day to feed this village?

● Tribes had different hair styles. Describe a Pawnee man's hair style.

● The idea for this story came from a true happening in Pawnee history called the Battle of Massacre Canyon. It marked the final communal buffalo hunt for the Pawnee. Read about this event.

● Complete the following sentences:
   a. Wearing tanned leather clothes feels like_____.
   b. The ceiling of an earth lodge looks like _____.
   c. My favorite way to cook corn is _____. With what did Elzvee eat corn soup?

THE ARTS

● The Pawnees sang songs to things they held as sacred. Some were sung in ceremonies, some while they did their work, and some to entertain and teach children.

Write a song or poem about something that is important to you.

GATHERING INFORMATION

● Corn was very important to the Pawnee. Gather recipes for preparing corn. List places where you can find recipes?

> Recipe books (in the library
> > and at home)
> Magazines
> Newspapers (in food section)
> Internet
> Mothers, relatives, and friends
> Backs of food packages!

Can you think of others?

Now that you have found all those good recipes, make a "Corny" Class Cook Book.

THE BEST I CAN BE

● Grandmother reminded Elzvee that "...breath is the blessing of life. Words are spoken with breath so they are sacred and must be used with care."

With these wise words in mind, try this activity. Every student in the room needs to write his or her name across the top of a sheet of paper. Pass each sheet around the room. As a name comes to you, write something about that person that you like. When everyone has written something **on every sheet**, return the paper to the name at the top.

You will treasure learning what good things people think about you!

NEVER, NEVER say words that hurt another person!